Santa's Surprise Sleigh

Written by Susan Karnovsky

Illustrated by Kathleen Dunne

Published by Playmore Inc., Publishers, 58 Main Street, 2ⁿᵈ Floor, Hackensack, N.J. 07601
and Waldman Publishing Corp., 570 Seventh Avenue, New York, N.Y. 10018
Copyright © MCMXCII Playmore Inc., Publishers
and Waldman Publishing Corp., New York, New York
All rights reserved
Conforms to ASTM F963-96a and EN71
Printed in China

It was a few days before Christmas. Hank's grandfather - whom everybody called Mr. Fix-It - was looking for the box of Christmas tree decorations.

"It's here somewhere," he muttered.

Oh Grandpa, Hank thought. *You'll never find anything in this pile of junk.*

"Why here it is," his grandfather said, "right where I put it on Abe Lincoln's desk."

"Abe Lincoln's desk?! Come on, Grandpa," Hank said.

"This was his desk...when he was a little boy!"

"And this little wooden horse was made by one of Santa's elves."

Hank hated the stories his grandpa made up about the junk in his barn...especially the stories about Christmas.

Grandpa never stopped telling stories. Sometimes Hank wished his family didn't live on his grandpa's farm.

"Maybe Santa Claus will be back for his sleigh blade this year," Grandpa continued.

Hank had heard enough. "Come on, Grandpa. Cut it out. I know better! So don't make up stories for me, okay?"

"Okay," his grandpa softly replied.

Early the next morning Hank watched his Grandfather trudge out to the barn. It was snowing pretty hard, but his Grandpa didn't even seem to notice. Sometimes Hank worried about him.

By the time Hank reached the barn, Grandpa Fix-It was already inside, digging under a pile of junk, trying to pull out an old rusty sleigh runner.

"This here belongs to Santa. Gotta polish it up," he said.

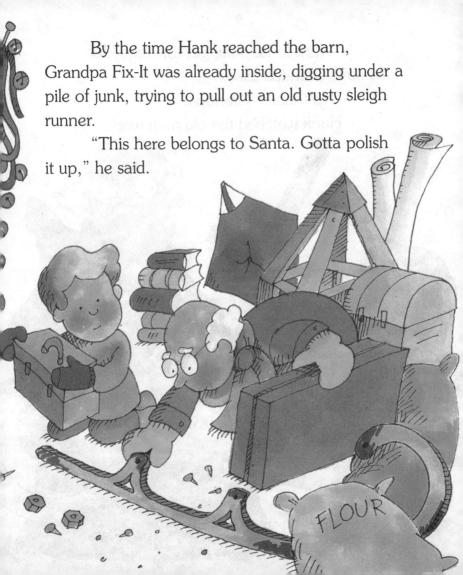

"Want to help me get this ready for Santa?" Grandpa asked.

"No thanks, Grandpa."

Hank watched the old man work.

Grandpa Fix-It scraped off the rust and then polished the old fashioned runner until it gleamed like new silver.

"See how the tip curls up?" his grandpa said. "Must have taken some elves a pretty hour to make that!"

Grandpa worked on the blade all day. He was working so hard, he didn't hear the dinner bell ring.

"Grandpa," Hank called.

But he didn't come in. Grandpa Fix-It was polishing the blade as if he expected someone to show up for it any moment.

"He'll freeze out there working on that runner," Hank's mother said. "There's a snow-storm!

"You know how he is once he starts on a project," Hank's aunt chimed in. "There's no stopping him."

Hank's father agreed. "I'll go out and get him."

But Grandpa was
gone. So was the blade.
Only the lantern
remained.

Hank's father returned to the house. He was worried.

"Grandpa's not out there. And he's not in the barn."

Hank and his uncle and dad went back outside to search for him.

"Grandpa!" Hank called. But his shouts were muffled by the snowfall.

Hank looked all around the stump for some clue. For a moment Hank thought he saw hoof prints and sleigh tracks in the snow near the barn. But the snowstorm was getting worse. It was hard to be sure.

Everyone returned to the house.

His father was talking on the phone to the police when Hank thought he heard the sound of distant sleighbells.

Hank looked out the window. Could those be reindeer out there? No.

Was that someone out there with a red and white outfit and a white beard? It couldn't be!

Did he hear laughter? Sleighbells?
Hank rubbed his eyes and peered through
the snow.

A few moments later, Grandpa Fix-It came
in, twinkle-eyed and red-cheeked.

"Blade works fine," Grandpa said as he took his coat off.

"Finished it just in time, too. Got me a little sample ride. Santa's right pleased!" he muttered.

Everyone was so happy to see grandpa
that they didn't pay any attention to what he was
saying. Only Hank noticed the sleigh outside.
And only Hank heard the merry Ho! ho! ho! that
faded off, up into the winter sky.

Grandpa and Hank smiled secretly at each other. From that moment on, Hank knew his Grandpa Fix-It was the most special grandpa anyone could ask for.